The Selfish Giant

A Story about Being Unselfish

Retold by Justine A. Ciovacco
Illustrated by Len Ebert

Famous Fables

Reader's Digest Young Families

Once upon a time, a group of children happily
played in the beautiful garden of a castle. They had
been playing there every day for as long as they could
remember. Each day they entered through a hole in the
stone wall that surrounded the property.

The garden was covered with thick, green grass, and colorful flowers all around. Trees were bursting with pink and pearly white blossoms. Birds sang to one another from the tree branches as the children played below.

"What a wonderful place for games!" shouted one boy to his friend.

"I can't think of a thing that's better than playing here," she giggled.

As the children's laughter drifted through the air, a giant came trudging up a nearby hill. He was on his way home to the castle. He had been away for a very long time. Now the giant was returning to the place where he had lived from the time when he was a baby giant. He wanted some peace and quiet.

"I don't want noise," grumbled the giant. "I especially don't want children playing on my property! I want to be alone."

The giant stomped through his castle and into the garden.

"Get out of my garden!" he shouted. As the children ran away, the giant called out, "No one is allowed to be in my garden except me!"

The giant quickly made a sign and stuck it outside the stone wall. Then he placed a pile of rocks in front of the hole to keep the children out.

"Now I'll be rid of those noisy children," the giant said. "I don't want to hear or see anyone in my garden!"

The children stood quietly on the other side of the wall. They were sad. They had no other place to play that would be as much fun as the giant's garden.

Each day the giant sat in his garden and enjoyed its beauty. But within a few days, the trees began to lose their blossoms and leaves. The flowers dropped their petals. The birds sang less and less. But the giant never noticed.

From time to time, the giant heard scraping sounds coming from the rocks he had put in front of the hole in the wall. He growled every time he heard the noise.

"Get away!" he would shout. "This garden is mine!"

But the children didn't give up. They returned every day, hoping that the giant would be nicer, or that he would leave on a giant adventure.

Soon the giant's garden was a very different place. The trees were bare. The flowers were gone. The few patches of grass that were left were dried out. And the birds no longer sang.

The giant looked out of his window and thought for a long time.

"I have my peace and quiet. I have my garden to myself. Yet I feel empty . . . almost bare, like the branches of my trees," he said to himself.

He wondered why his garden was so bare while the trees and flowers he could see on the other side of the wall were still in full bloom.

Then the giant heard the children outside his wall. As usual, he shouted, "Go away! This garden is mine."

The next day, the giant awoke to the sound of voices. He ran to the window. In a far corner of the garden, he could see two children climbing a tree. And the tree was full of leaves and blossoms! It was the only one that wasn't bare. The giant also saw a small boy trying to climb another tree, but the boy was too small to reach a branch.

The giant ran downstairs. "I'll teach these children to stay away from my garden," he growled.

As soon as the bigger children saw the giant, they ran away. But the small boy never noticed him. All his attention was focused on trying to climb that tree.

As the giant approached the small boy, he
thought about when he was a young giant, and small
for his age. He remembered having trouble climbing
up that very tree. His big brother always lifted him onto
a branch.

The giant picked up the small boy and lifted him
onto a branch.

"Sometimes we all need a bit of help," the giant
told the little boy in a loud but kind voice.

The little boy smiled at the giant.

Suddenly, the bare tree began to show new leaves and blossoms. Once again, the treetop bloomed with pink and pearly white flowers.

The small boy thanked the giant for his help. "You are not as scary and mean as everyone says," he told the giant. "I'd like to come back tomorrow. May I?" the boy asked.

The giant nodded. He realized that he had been very selfish with his garden. "Yes," said the giant, "and bring your friends."

The next day, the small boy crawled through the hole in the wall. The other children followed. Once they started playing, laughing, and shouting, the whole garden started blooming. The giant met them in the garden. He was smiling. Everyone was happy.

"It's not good to be selfish. In fact, being selfish is very lonely," the giant said. "From now on, I will always share my garden."

"And we will come back and play every day!" the children promised.

Famous Fables, Lasting Virtues
Tips for Parents

Now that you've read The Selfish Giant, *use these pages as a guide in teaching your child the virtues in the story. By talking about the story and engaging in the suggested activities, you can help your child develop good judgment and a strong moral character.*

About Being Unselfish

It's natural for young children to want to keep things for themselves, especially during the early stages of growing up. But children do learn with experience that sharing doesn't mean giving up something forever. Children need guidance, though, to understand why being selfish hurts people's feelings. They also need help understanding how, in the long term, being selfish will also hurt themselves. The following thoughts may help your child learn to appreciate the value of being unselfish:

1. *Some benefits of sharing.* When you have an opportunity to have a discussion with your child, ask him if he can come up with reasons why sharing is a good thing to do. For example, a toy might be more fun to play with if he and his friend play with it together, even if that means taking turns with the toy. The friend might even find a new way to play with the toy.

2. *Sharing can start a friendship.* When you have something that you can share, think about who would be happiest to share it with you. Imagine if there was a child who didn't have many friends at school. Being unselfish and sharing something with that person would make him feel good. It's always nice to share with people who are already your friends, but sometimes you can make friends by being unselfish.

3. *Unselfishness is its own reward.* As adults, we know that being unselfish makes a person feel better about himself, but this is something children learn over time. The more your child shares something or helps a member of the family, a friend, a classmate, a neighbor, or someone in need, the sooner he will understand this on his own. Being unselfish is truly rewarding. Look for opportunities for you and your child to help others.